FREE BIRDS

Shreya Konkimalla

Copyright © 2017 Shreya Konkimalla

This book is a work of fiction. Names, characters, places, and incidents are either product of the author's imagination or are used fictitiously. Any resemblance to actual persons, living or dead, events or locales is entirely coincidental.

Table of Contents

A Note from the Author

History has its highs and lows. It can be dark at times and brilliant at others. It is not always sunshine; it can be a flood of tears. And every single place on Earth has some beautiful, lovely history as well as grim, bleak tales. This story is about one of those grim and bleak parts of history.

Before the year 1950, India had a *caste system* where *untouchability* was widespread. In this system, people belonged to one of four castes, or classes. The higher you were in the caste, the better off you were in life. At the top of the caste were the *Brahmins*. Brahmins were the religious leaders and teachers. One rung below the Brahmins were the *Kshatriyas*, who were the warriors and people of the royal families. One step down from the Kshatriyas were the *Vaishyas*. Vaishyas were merchants, or people who sold and traded things. Then came the *Sudras*. They were the workers and servants.

Finally, at the very bottom of the caste, were the *Dalits*, or the *untouchables*. They were so inferior that they were not even part of the caste system. The untouchables did the dirty work; work that no one else wanted to do. They had to do anything from sweeping streets to cleaning human waste. They were constantly oppressed and humiliated by all the other castes. It was considered polluting and inauspicious to touch them or even step in their shadow! That's why they were called untouchables.

Even though India abolished untouchability, it is still prevalent in certain parts of India.

This story is set in the 1700s, when India was divided into many different kingdoms and ruled by local kings.

Prologue
June 12th, 1751

"Please. I beg you, kind sir, please help me!" the man howled.

The fire raged on, showing no mercy to anything in its path. The yellow and red flames licked the edges of the wooden frame as it slowly charred to black, sending billowing smoke into the air. A column of wood fell on the man's leg. He screamed in pain. Ram looked over at the crippled man and ran to his side.

"Guard! Come here! I need help! Leave that thing to die," yelled princess Aishani, beckoning him over. Ram looked over to her. She was standing amidst the flames, searching for a way out. Her *sari* was flowing around her, twinkling in the light of the fire. She looked at her surroundings. Strands of her brown hair floated around her face as she desperately looked around. Her diamond jewelry shone brightly, and she touched her head to make sure her crown was still in place on top of her head. Its daintiness fit the princess's elegant nature, even in the fiery madness.

"Come here *now!*" she demanded, her gray-green eyes filled with anger.

Ram pulled the man from under the wood and started running. "I'll come back for you, princess! I promise!" he shouted back to her. He ran to the doorway, which was wide open. The door wasn't there anymore, and remnants of it were strewn about outside. He kept running and set the man down where many others already lay, coughing and sputtering.

"Thank you. You are my god," thanked the man in a raspy voice. His hollow cheeks and chin were covered with gray stubble. All he wore were old rags that were tattered in many places.

Ram ran back to the palace and through the doorway to Aishani. "What is wrong with you, you ignorant idiot? How dare you ignore me?" Aishani sputtered, her eyes tearing up with smoke and anger.

Ram jumped over fallen columns to reach her. Aishani was sitting down now, a bit dazed. Ram scooped her up and ran out of the palace, gasping for fresh air to clear out the smoke that had gathered in his lungs. Within moments, the wooden structure collapsed in a fiery blaze. He ran to the front yard and was about to set Aishani down on the grass next to the others.

"Bring her to the tent," King Dayananda bellowed.

"Yes, sir," Ram said, bowing. He scanned the surroundings and spotted a white tent. He looked back at all the injured people on the emerald-green lawn. Obviously, none of the lower castes would be allowed in the tents. He saw the flap in one of the tents and ducked in. There were rows of blue cots and a little washing table with some herbs and medicines laid out on top. A slight breeze floated into the tent, making the flap sway gently, peacefully. By the looks of it, no one could have imagined such an awful scene right outside. He carefully placed Aishani onto one of the cots.

"I'm so sorry, princess," Ram whispered. Aishani looked deeply into his eyes for a minute. Then she slapped him across the face. Ram's hand shot up to his stinging cheek and he looked at Aishani in shock.

"Do you know what you just did?" she asked. Ram looked at the ground. "I repeat; do you know what you just did?" she asked, a little louder. Still, he did not answer.

"You just saved an untouchable first, instead of me – the queen's sister! Don't you know that I am so much more important than an untouchable? Do you know what the king will do because of what you just did? He'll kill you," she said, her eyes full of rage, "and he'll show you no mercy. And if he doesn't kill you, then my sister will make sure you're punished."

"But princess, that man surely would have died if I hadn't saved him first. His life was in grave danger and he couldn't move because he was crippled," Ram stammered.

Her eyes blazing as fiercely as the fire burning outside, Aishani exclaimed, "It doesn't matter! You are ordered to help the royal family before anyone else!"

Just as Aishani finished her sentence, King Dayananda marched into the tent.

"What happened? Why is she injured? Why did she come out last, after an untouchable?" King Dayananda asked. Ram looked at Aishani, then at Dayananda. From the corner of his eye, he saw Aishani staring at the two of them, a frown forming on her delicate face.

"Sir," Ram said, looking at Aishani, "it is my fault

that the princess is injured. I saved the untouchable first, because he surely would have died if I hadn't. He was engulfed in flames, sir. I *had* to save him first. If I hadn't, he surely would have died right there."

Aishani started to say something, but King Dayananda raised a hand to silence her. His eyes flickered with anger; his jaw clenched firmly. Ram could hear him breathing heavily at first, then more steady, slow breaths.

In a deadly calm voice, King Dayananda said, "Well, we can't have you doing that again, can we? My military does not need a person like you. I will show people what happens to traitors who go against the law. You will be killed first thing in the morning. You can say your goodbyes tonight. My soldiers will come and get you after the sky turns dark." Ram stared at the king, unable to move or speak. "Oh, and one more thing," the king continued. "Since you clearly don't care enough about your own life, your family should suffer the consequences, too. From this moment forward, they will be branded untouchables."

With that, King Dayananda marched out of the room, his velvet robe flowing behind him. He stopped just outside the tent and took a minute to adjust his crown, the jewels glinting in the sunlight, reflecting power and hate; power over everyone lower than him, hate for everyone lower than him. Bellowing orders to a group of guards, he marched off.

Ram stood frozen like a statue, too stunned to move. His gaze followed King Dayananda. "Oh, no," he whispered. Aishani looked shocked too, and did not say a word. "I didn't know he would do anything to my family. I have two young children! What will happen to their lives?" Ram said, his face etched with worry.

Aishani's eyes filled with concern. "Why did you do this?" she cried. "Now your poor family will have to suffer the consequences of your poor decisions!"

"I didn't do anything wrong," Ram said quietly. "I helped the person who was most in need. He was going to die, princess. I couldn't just leave him there. It doesn't matter what his caste is. I'm terrified of what will happen to my family, but I know what I did was right."

Aishani shoulders slumped. "Your family will have to endure so much pain now."

"Yes, but there's nothing I can do now," Ram said,

standing on shaky legs and unsteadily making his way to the exit.

"I'm worried about all the suffering your family will go through," Aishani whispered.

"What do you know about suffering, Princess Aishani?" Ram snapped before he could think.

She looked away and clenched her teeth. They were both silent for several moments. "I've seen my fair share of it when I'm outside the palace," she mumbled stiffly.

Ram's mind was a thousand miles away. His face darkened as he realized what this would mean for his family. He had seen so many untouchables begging for money by the marketplace and along the streets just to get some food. Most people avoided them and kept their children as far from them as possible. Ram often felt sorry for the untouchables and wondered what their stories were. He would drop a coin or two into their empty, leathery hands. After he died, would his family be the ones on the street begging for coins to get a bite of food? "I need to go home now," Ram said finally.

"Wait," Aishani said. Ram paused.

"I owe you. You did save my life. I was angry, but honestly, I would have died out there if it weren't for you. I can tell a man like you cares *a lot* about your family. Your wife and children...they must matter an awful lot to you. And what will they do with you not there to take care of them? They'll be in bad shape. I will try to help them somehow. I owe it to you," she said.

"Thank you," he whispered, a single tear falling down his cheek.

Ram trudged home, wondering how he would explain to his family what had happened. Would he have to just say that he was going to die? Or explain the events that led up to that decision? Or did they already know? His daughter, Navya, was only eight, and his son, Rohit, ten. Would they even understand what was happening? He looked down at his black shoes covered in mud, his navy blue uniform covered in ashes. A fresh red cut ran down his arm. How come he hadn't felt it until now?

Even after all he'd gone through and the lives he'd saved, he'd done something wrong. But had he really? It was the worst feeling, he thought, looking down at the ground. Even though he knew in his heart he did the right thing, he started doubting himself. Why else would the king punish him? *Am I bad? Am I wrong? Do I deserve this punishment?*

With these thoughts whirling around in his head, he walked back home with his head hanging low. When he got to his doorstep, he couldn't take it anymore. He fell to the ground and punched it over and over again. He screamed in pain and cried. He sat there crying into his hands as he heard the curtains rustle at the front door. His sweet daughter rushed to his side and hugged him. Knowing he could no longer protect her, he gently ran his fingers through her long hair.

"Papa, why are you crying?" she asked, her voice filled with concern as she peered into his eyes.

He saw love, bravery and confidence in Navya's eyes, all natural for their Kshatriya caste. After all, they were the warriors who protected the kingdom, but that same confidence would get her into a lot of trouble as an untouchable.

"I love you, Navi, I love you so much," Ram whispered in her ear as he hugged her tightly. "Never, ever forget that."

Inside, he somehow mustered the courage to tell his family what had happened, but to him it was all a blur. There were hugs and tears. Lots of tears.

And then when the sky turned a dark blue and the stars began to twinkle outside, there was a knock at the door. Ram opened the door and looked outside. A carriage awaited him. He looked back at his family helplessly. Navi clung to the bottom of his coat, looking up at him, tears streaming down her small, innocent face.

"Papa! Papa, don't leave," she cried.

He tried to step outside, but she hung on tight. He kneeled next to her. Gulping in air, he fought back sobs and forced a smile. "I'll never leave you, Navi. Ever. I'll always be here," he said, pointing to her heart. "In there. I will help you when you are in need, and I will show you the right paths to take, my dear. I'll never leave your side. I promise you that."

Then he reached around his neck and pulled off his gold chain and hat. He carefully placed the necklace around her neck and put the hat on top of her head. He smiled and hugged her tightly. "There. Now you will always have a piece of me. I love you, Navi."

Without looking back, Ram turned and walked to the carriage. Saanvi, his wife, held their children close. They watched until the carriage was a small speck on the horizon, then watched some more, unable to move. At last, Saanvi and Rohit slowly made their way inside.

But Navya kept watching until dawn approached and the sky lit up again with pastel pinks and oranges. She watched as the sun began to rise. The trees swayed in the breeze. Lifting her hand up towards the last place she'd seen her father, she waved.

"I love you, Papa," she whispered into the wind.

Chapter 1
Four Years Later

I try to listen to the teacher ramble on with her lessons. I know I'm supposed to listen, because it is very hard to be in a school if you are like me – an untouchable.

I look around the school, gripping the edge of the log I am sitting on. Our school is under an old *banyan* tree. The roots of the tree hang overhead. Children of every age are packed into a small area, trying to stay away from the hot sun, yet everyone stays as far away as possible from me. I actually don't hate it. After all, I get a whole lot of space to myself.

I peer through the leaves at the hot, burning sun above us. The leaves and branches of the tree usually keep us cool, but they're not doing a good job today. My hair sticks to the back of my neck in the sweltering heat. I slump and stare towards the front of the class, lost in thought. The teacher drones on about math and tells us to write a math problem on our slates. I think about my chores and whether I'll have to go on my long walk to wash clothes today.

There is no point of going to school as an untouchable. Nothing I learn here is going to help me do great things as long as I'm an untouchable. I've tried to convince Ma to let me work with her so we can earn more money, but she forces me to go to school.

No untouchables go to school. They all work with their parents. I'm in here because I used to go to school before I became an untouchable. Ma used to be friends with the teacher. They were the ones who decided to make a school for all the children. Usually girls didn't go to school, but since they created this school, they decided the rules. Ma used to be a teacher too, but that was before we became untouchables. Then Ma wasn't "fit" to teach anymore. The teacher allowed Rohit and I to continue coming here, somewhat reluctantly.

"Navya? Hello?" the teacher says, interrupting my daydream.

"Oh, sorry! What is it Madam...?" I ask, scrambling to stand up and forgetting her name for an instant.

She shakes her head at me in disgust. "What's the answer to the problem? I've asked you five times now," she says, tapping her foot impatiently.

I stare down at my feet in their tattered sandals. A few classmates laugh at me, while others shake their heads in disgust. Some of them just ignore me completely.

"I...I don't know," I stammer. I sit back down and rest my head in my hands, waiting for her to tell me to come up to the front for a beating. Instead, she just clucks her tongue and continues teaching.

Finally, after what seems like days, the teacher says, "Well, we are done with school for the day. After the break, we will pick up where we left off. Remember to study your lessons over the break. I don't want any of you falling behind."

I quickly grab my slate and chalk next to me and start walking away, hoping that the teacher won't see me and ask me to stay behind. Just as I take a step out of the shade of the trees, relieved to see my foot lit up with the sunlight, she calls my name.

"Navya? Can you come here?" she asks. I stop and close my eyes. *Oh why, oh why, couldn't I have walked faster?* I wonder in dismay.

I turn around and plaster a smile on my face. "Yes, Radha madam?" I ask as sweetly as possible.

"Can you come over here?" she asks, a steely edge in her voice. Slowly, ever so slowly, I walk towards her and wait for her to do something. I see a long wooden stick in her two hands. *Will she yell at me? I* wonder. *Slap me? Beat me with the stick? What could she possibly do?*

"Navya, do you realize that you are really lucky to be in school? You should use your time in class well. Can't you just pay attention in class?"

"What do you mean, 'I'm lucky to be in school?'" I ask a little too quickly. I feel my fake smile fade away and my voice turn to stone.

"Most of your kind don't get to go to school like you do," she says. "They have to work all day." Her eyes are narrowed and a look of disdain covers her face. "You don't belong here, especially if you don't pay attention."

Her hatred for me, for "my kind", makes me weak at the knees and my legs feel like jelly. I fight back tears and lift my chin, determined to not let her see me cry. "Because I'm an untouchable?" I ask. "I know, and you should know that I'm trying my best to pay attention in class. But since I'm an," I point to myself and accent the next word, "*untouchable*...I have a lot of other things on my

17

mind."

The teacher stares at me. "Everyone has their own problems, but at school, I want you to be focused. It's not *my* fault that you're an untouchable," she says coldly.

"What do you mean, it's not your fault?" I cry out, unable to hold back emotion any longer. "Does that mean that it's someone else's fault?"

She doesn't reply, just continues to burn holes in my face with her angry eyes.

"Are you saying it is my Papa's fault, then?" I demand, not caring how my words come out. "Is it? Is it his fault that I'm an untouchable and have these problems? Because he saved two people instead of one? Is that what you mean? And what about all the other people of my caste? You think they chose to be untouchables? Is it their fault? Is that what you think? And don't even start to tell me 'Everyone has their own problems.' Don't you know how hard life is for an untouchable?" I yell, breathing heavily.

She puts her hands on her hips and looks at me. I can feel my face flush as the rage boils inside of me, daring to overflow.

"That —" she starts, but I interrupt her.

"Don't treat me like I'm different from everyone else because I'm an untouchable. You can say whatever you want about my behavior, but don't say that I'm lucky to be here or I should be grateful that I'm in a school," I tell her, trying to steady my voice.

And with that, I spin on my heel and run way. Tears sting my eyes as I try to fight them off. My sandals make a crunching sound against the gravel and I feel the sharpness of the rocks digging into my feet; the flimsy, tattered old sandals offer no protection.

"Navya! Come back here; we are not done with this conversation!" she calls after me, her voice a little less sharp than before.

I look back over my shoulder at her. Her hair is pulled into a perfect up-do and she wears a cotton navy blue sari. Her sandals have no holes in them. Instead, they shine. She's not a Brahmin, but she is much better off than I am.

I turn my head and start running home, but not before someone gets in my way.

"Poor little Navya. So sad and alone!" Rita teases

in a baby voice. Rita's friends cackle along with her. "Oh! Are you *crying*? Can't you make it a day without embarrassing yourself?" Rita laughs.

I look at the ground. My face is red, my feet hurt and I am tired. So tired. All I want is to go home and forget this day every happened. "Leave me alone," I say quietly.

"What did you say?" Rita asks.

"Leave. Me. ALONE!" I yell into her face. I'm sick of her making fun of me. I'm sick of school. I am so sick of everything I go through each day. So what do I do then? I do the most stupid thing I can think of: I slap her. Yes, Rita; I slap her. Right across her pretty little face, leaving a bright red handprint on her right cheek. And oh, did it feel good.

"You little...do you know what you have just done? My papa is going to come and beat you up, you little…!" she screams, fire burning in her eyes. She kicks my feet, sending me tumbling to the ground. Her friends join in, throwing kicks. I look up as the blue sky turns gray. They don't stop until Rita's dad comes.

"Rita! What is going on here?" he demands, trying to break up the group.

"She slapped me! Forget about that; she *touched* me!" she whines, pointing at me.

Her dad studies my dark brown eyes and rounded nose. I can tell he's trying to figure out who I am. Then it clicks and I can almost see the lightbulb go off in his head. "Ram's daughter," he whispers to himself, but I hear it. He shakes his head, almost pitying me.

"What did you say?" Rita asks.

"Nothing. Come back, Rita. She's not worth your time," he mutters, his eyes still locked on my face. Rita runs to her papa and her friends follow her. He puts an arm around her shoulder and leads her away to their house. Right before the turn in the road, he looks back.

The sunlight that was present a moment ago is now completely hidden behind angry clouds. It starts to rain, and I struggle to get on my feet. I pick up my things strewn in the mud and limp back to my house. The rain soaks me to the bone as I shiver and whimper, tears spilling down my face, and I can't tell my tears from the rain.

Usually, I love when it rains. That's the only time that my older brother and I can play outside without anyone judging us or giving us funny looks. Today, the rain does not improve my mood.

As I limp in the rain, I pass nice houses with pretty flowers in their beautiful gardens. I stare at them. We used to live in a house like these ones. I had my own bedroom. I think about that now.

"This is your new room now," Papa says, opening the big wooden door to a large room.

In the center lies a huge bed. A colorful blanket lies at the foot of the bed. On one side of the bed is a teak *dresser. On top of it is a vase filled with fresh flowers.*

I run up to the bed and crawl up onto it, standing in the center. I start jumping on the bed, laughing and falling into the soft mattress. My curls bounce around my face. Papa stands near the door, grinning.

"So now I will sleep over here? Not next to Rohit anymore?" I ask.

"Yes," he replies, still smiling.

"What if I get scared?" I ask.

"Then you can come get me," Papa says, walking over to me.

He picks me up and twirls me in circles and we both laugh.

As I continue walking, the nice houses turn into

crumbling houses that are falling apart. Then come the small shacks made from scraps of wood and stones. Children my age and younger play in the mud and dirt. Some look around for food in carts that were abandoned in the rain. They are all dressed in rags and frayed clothing.

Finally, I am almost home. As I pass the hut closest to ours, I see someone lying against the door. I limp closer and see that it's our neighbor. Her eyes stare into the distance and aren't focused on me. I kneel next to her.

"Aunty, are you alright?" I ask, shaking her a little.

Her dull eyes move to my face and she finally comes back to reality. "I was in a better place," she says, frowning at me. I rinse my hands in the rain, cup a hand to collect water in and bring it to her lips. She shivers. She tries to get up and falls back down, so I help her regain her balance. I guide her inside her hut and help her peel of her wet *chunni* and wrap a dry blanket around her shoulders. Then I take out the food I was supposed to have for lunch: two pieces of cooked chicken with a few beans. My stomach grumbles, but I mash it up and feed her my meal. After she's finished it all, I get up.

More alert now and in better spirits, she studies me up close and asks, "Did someone do this to you, Navya?"

"What do you mean?" I say.

"I may be starving, but I'm not stupid. Look at yourself, child," she says. I hang my head and look at my rain-soaked sandals.

Moving towards the door, I mutter, "I have to go."

"Just remember: don't let them get to you. You are so much stronger than them, *beta*," she coos. I give her a weary smile and go back outside, where the rain has now slowed to a drizzle. I reach our little shed and bend down to get inside. Ma rushes up to me, her forehead creased and eyebrows furrowed with worry. "Where were you, Navi? Your brother came much earlier than you did. You should have been here…" she says, looking at me closely.

I can tell she's studying my red cheeks and the scrapes all over my body. She doesn't ask any questions, just pulls me into a hug. She waves me over to our washroom – a pail, cup and stool behind a curtain – and I see that the pail is filled with hot water, a delightful treat. She closes the curtains and lets me have my privacy. I peel off my clothes and sandals and sit on the stool, so relieved to finally be home. I close my eyes.

In my reverie, I imagine we live in a huge, sprawling palace. I have a room full of art materials and famous paintings. My brother, Rohit, has a room full of books all to himself. Ma flits about in her spacious kitchen and cooks anything and everything, aided by a fleet of cooks. And Papa is with us, holding me tightly in his arms, hugging me with his strong arms, telling me everything will be all right.

A noise snaps me back to reality and the dream world I've created in my mind fades away. No, that is not my life. I live in a shed made of flimsy wood. Our roof is made of bundled-up sticks. I have one small paint brush I found tossed in the gutter. Rohit has one book he found in the dumpster that he's read more than a hundred times. Ma has a small clay stove in the corner of our shed that she huddles around to make the little food we can get. And Papa...Papa is gone.

I open my eyes and a tear slides down my face. Papa is gone.

<u>Chapter 2</u>

The water is starting to get cold, so I pour it over my body and use the small scraps of soap nuts left to clean myself. I rub the last morsels of it into my curly, dirt-encrusted hair. I sigh, wishing that getting soap nuts was easy and inexpensive as I quickly wash myself with the rest of the water in the pail.

Using a small rag to dry myself, I see that Ma has set out some clean clothes for me on a dry brick. I assume she went to the river to clean them. I slip into an old blouse and *langa* that Ma gave me as a gift last month. They are nice and looked new, but when I asked, she wouldn't tell me where she got them from.

A slight breeze stirs the curtain and makes my hair flap in my face. I pat it down and then come out of our washroom. Ma jumps out of her chair and looks at me. She makes me sit down on our old, rickety chair and inspects all my injuries. She sighs, getting out our ancient medicine kit wrapped in a graying old rag. She cleans my wounds and uses every last bit of her medicine on me. "Ma, why are you using all that medicine? It's so expensive! We can't afford any more." I say.

"I'll make some more; I'm not going to buy any. I'll find some herbs and plants in the forest to make the medicine. A friend told me how to make it myself," she soothes. I sigh and Ma packs up her medicine kit at last. She nods to our little sleeping corner and I limp over there, falling into my bed, completely exhausted from the day. We had to make these beds when we moved. I had packed some straw to make a mattress and covered it with a blanket Ma bought for me, and covered it with a quilt she gave me for warmth.

I close my eyes, huddled in the warmth of my bed. I hear Ma collapse into the chair and sigh. I open my eyes a tiny bit and see that she's rubbing her face and rocking back and forth on the chair. She opens her eyes and begins to cry.

"Ram, why did you leave me? The children need you, Ram," she whispers, as she squeezes her eyes shut. "Navya...she is just like you. I don't want her to get in trouble like you did. I can't handle one more family loss, Ram. I simply can't." Ma gets out of the chair and walks to the wall, looking at the portrait of Papa. I smile, remembering how jittery

Papa was when he got that portrait done.

"Stop moving! You are going to look like a pig in the painting if you keep moving around," Ma scolds, laughing.

"I'm sorry. I can't help it! This stool is just so uncomfortable," Papa says, adjusting himself again.

The painter smiles, shaking his head at my silly family. While Papa is getting his portrait done, we look on from the side. Rohit, as usual, has his nose in a book, his face wrinkled in concentration. I look up at him and tug his kurta, *trying to get his attention. "Rohit! Play with me!" I whine.*

Rohit gets irritated and shoos me away. I start laughing and tugging at his kurta again. Finally, he puts his book down and picks me up. I grin, happy to get my way.

Finally, Papa's painting is done. We gather around the artist to inspect his work, my brother carrying me so I can see it, too. The artist perfectly captured the intelligent glint in Papa's eyes and his kind smile. His hair looks ruffled, but still soft. It's stunning.

The memory drifts away and I think about how different our life was then, how Rohit had books and we had nice clothes. We were carefree.

I realize I must have dozed off when Rohit wakes

me up.

"Navya, get up!" Rohit yells, shaking me violently.

"Okay, okay, I'm getting up! Calm down. I was resting. Why do you want me up?" I say, putting my hands up in the air.

"We got a mysterious package, addressed to "Ram's Family". Ma told me we have to wait for you to get up to open it. I want to open it now!" he exclaims.

I groan, pushing myself up onto my elbows. I collapse immediately as pain shoots up my arms.

"Owww," I moan, lying back down.

Rohit helps me up and lets me sit in our chair. Then he grabs the package and sits on the floor next to me. Ma joins us moments later. She looks at me, worry filling her eyes. Rohit doesn't notice and starts to open the package. I can't stand the suspense, so I grab the package from him. In it, there is a letter, written on fancy stationery. I begin to read:

Dear Friends,

Ram once saved my life. He was a kind man and he helped me when I was helpless. It has taken me years to find you, and finally I know where you live. I am so sorry for your loss, and I know there is nothing I can do to make up for what happened, but I feel the need to help you in some way, as I owe it to Ram. This is all I could do for now. I hope it's enough.

Sincerely,

A Dear Friend

I pass the letter around to Rohit and Ma and they read it, huddled together. Then they hand it back to me. I tilt the package slightly and a handful of coins slide into my lap. I look at them in awe. Ma stares at them, blinking her eyes a few times in wonder and disbelief.

"Who could it be from?" I wonder aloud. "Rohit, who brought this to us?"

"I don't know. I found it by the door when I came back from bringing water," Rohit said.

Ma looks over the letter several times.

"I'm grateful to whoever sent this. These coins can help us a lot. We can buy food and even help our neighbor, who is sick. We must keep these coins safe," she whispers.

She goes to make us dinner while I figure out a place to hide the coins. I look at my bed, thinking of an idea. I could hide them in the straw bed, below the blanket, so no one could see them. Yes, that's it. I get to work and, when I finish, Ma nods in approval, not saying a word.

My stomach grumbles as Ma sets up three steaming hot bowls of food on the floor. She ushers us to the mat. My brother follows as we sit down and look at what's in our bowls. Today, we have a small ball of rice and lentils divided between us. I finish the meager portion of food in no time. I lick the bowl, wishing there was more. Unlike the three-course meals we used to have when Papa was around, now we only have two meals a day – if we're lucky.

My stomach still growls loudly. Ma looks at me and winces at the noise. I curse myself, wishing my stomach would shut up. Now Ma will feel bad. "Take my portion, Navi. I don't need it," Ma coaxes.

"No. Ma, please eat your portion. You need to be healthy, too," I say.

But she doesn't listen. Instead, she pushes it towards me. Wafts of the sweet and spicy lentils make my stomach grumble again. I close my eyes, trying to stop myself from eating the food.

"Ma, no. Please, eat it. Please," I plead. She shakes her head and then gets up and heads outside. I sigh and realize my brother is looking at Ma's food, too. I give him half and keep the other half for me. We both play with the food, guilt filling our stomachs. I try to take a bite, but I can't bring the food to my lips. My brother looks down at his feet. Anger cooks inside of me. Just one more handful of food for my family...

I limp outside the shed and see that the sun is setting. Puddles of reddish-brown water surround me. Teardrops of water fall from a soppy tree. I look around for Ma and find her near the garden.

Our garden is tiny; it has only a few plants that we grew from seeds. We hope that the rain will take care of them, but sometimes we have to get river water to nourish them. They usually don't do as well as we want them to, shriveling up into a pile of dried leaves. Yet somehow, some of them manage to survive. I take note of small onion, eggplant, chili and bean plants.

I see Ma bent over, trying to see if there is any more food left there. She plucks a few beans from one of the plants and bites into one, until she sees me from the corner of her eye and jumps up.

"Ma, I know you're hungry. You don't have to eat this raw food. Please come in and eat your portion. I'm really not hungry. Please," I say.

"Navya, I wish it was that easy, but day after day, I see my children starving, getting hurt, not getting enough sleep. Do you know how hard that is for me? I hate it, Navi. I just want to do one small thing to help, but you won't let me. Navi, I'll make it without eating my portion. I can't keep seeing you and Rohit like this. It hurts. I'd rather be hungry. And with your Papa gone –" she stops and breaks down, crying.

I rush towards her and hug her. I help her inside and sit her down on the chair, setting my bowl nearby. She calms down and picks up the bowl. With a trembling hand, she picks up some food and places it in her mouth. She closes her eyes and chews slowly. "Isn't it good?" I say. "See, even with the small amount of food we have, you manage to make everything taste good." I say, and she nods her head, a tight smile on her lips.

When she's finished, I pick the bowl up along with the others and place it in a pail with some other dirty dishes. I figure it's probably time to go wash them or we won't have anything clean to eat on.

I look back at Ma and see her staring off into the distance, hanging tightly onto the chair. Her loose black curls frame her face and fall just past her shoulders. I look into her hazel eyes, feeling their distance from me. They are so far away. I walk over to her. "It's been a long day," I whisper, tucking a strand of her hair behind her ear.

She nods, her eyes snapping back to reality, and looks at me ever so slightly. Her sadness weighs me down and I wish I could do something to make her feel better, to stop her pain. "I think we should get you into bed," I mutter, helping her up.

I lead her to her bed and lay her down gently. Remembering that she has no blanket, I cover her with my quilt. Her breathing steadies as she falls asleep.

I look up and see my brother looking at me. "You can take my blanket, Navi. I don't need it," he offers, holding his blanket out to me.

"It's fine, Rohit. Really." He climbs into bed, covering himself with his blanket. I look at his closed eyes until his breathing evens, too. I sit down on the ground near Ma and realize she's holding my hand. I try to pull away, but her hand won't budge. I lean against the wall and fall asleep to the hum of silence.

Chapter 3

I wake up to the hot sun beaming on my face, enveloping me in a blanket of warmth. Ma is still clutching my hand as if her life depends on it. Her eyes are closed and her hair is falling over her face. I look over to Rohit's bed and see that he isn't there. The blanket is kicked at the foot of the bed and his shoes are gone. I look around the shed and don't see him.

"Rohit! Rohit," I whisper, waiting for him to answer. He doesn't answer. The curtain to the washing area whooshes softly. Maybe he's using the washroom outside. Here, when we have to go to the washroom, we have to go in the forest. It's close by, so it usually doesn't cause a problem.

I wait for a while, but he still doesn't return. I sigh and decide to look for him. I slowly slide my hand out of Ma's grasp and walk outside our shed. I check the garden and surroundings. Seeing no sign of him, my heart starts to beat fast. Tha-thump. Tha-thump. Tha-thump.

Just then, I see Rohit streak through the bushes of

the forest. He comes rushing towards me with a bright smile on his face. His torn-up shoes pidder-padder on the ground, which is soft from last night's rain.

"Where were you?" I demanded. "You were gone for such a long time that I was worried!" He comes to a halt in front of me, panting and holding a basket in his hand.

"Forget that. Look what I found!" he exclaims. He pushes the basket towards me and I take it. I look inside and I see it spilling over with long, brown, bean-like pods and orangey-yellow fruit. *Tamarind* and *mangoes*?

"It doesn't matter! You can't just…just leave without telling anyone!" I exclaim. I put my hand on my hips, trying to look angry and annoyed at him, but my eyes keep drifting to the fruit. He gives me the basket and smiles.

"You're welcome," he says.

"How do you even know if these are safe to eat?" I ask nervously.

"Well, I already had some, so if it's not safe, then I'm pretty much dead," he laughs.

"Not. Funny. Don't you dare say that to Ma," I lecture.

He points to the basket. "Come on. Don't be a baby. Try some," he chides.

I sigh and pick up a piece of tamarind. I slowly remove the shell, revealing the sticky, gooey treat inside. Slowly, deliberately, I take a bite. I try to keep a straight face, but the corners of my mouth curl into a smile and I close my eyes, cherishing every morsel. I chew through the sweet and tangy fruit and spit out a seed. In no time, I'm finished with the treat and licking my fingers. I hold the black, glossy seeds in the palm of my hand.

"See? It's really good," he smiles. I take a mango and peel off the outer skin. I bite into the juicy flesh, and the sweet, intoxicating taste shoots through my entire being like a lightning bolt.

"This is so good," I muse, my mouth full of mango. I lick the mango juice off my fingers, wiping my hands on a leaf from a nearby tree and then head to the house. Ma sighs in relief as she sees us.

"I've been calling for you! You can't just leave like that!" she exclaims.

"I'm sorry, Ma, but Rohit just went somewhere into the forest and I was worried, so I went to look for him. I didn't mean to cause trouble," I explain.

"Ma, I got fruit!" Rohit cries. He holds out a mango and tamarind to Ma. She takes them and slowly eats them as we watch her normally rigid posture slowly soften. She smiles blissfully.

"Thank you, Rohit," she whispers.

With newfound vigor, I decide to finish my chores. "Ma, I'm going to the river to wash our dishes. We need clean dishes for the next meal. And I'll take our clothes, too. Most of them haven't been washed in weeks," I say.

"Oh, Navi, I forgot to tell you; I collected lots of rainwater, so we have fresh drinking water," she announces. I smile as I pack some ash and dry coconut rind on top of the dirty dishes. I head outside with one pail in each of my hands until I realize I have no soap nuts. I need to go buy some. I take two coins from Ma and trudge to the marketplace with my two pails and coins in hand. The marketplace is bustling with vendors selling their goods on carts. Everyone steers clear of me as I walk along.

I stop at a cart with soap nuts. The vendor ignores

me, staring at her nails and not looking up at me. I can tell she's annoyed. I set the two pails down and stare at her.

"Hello? I need some help!" I say loudly. Finally, the storekeeper looks up at me and her eyes narrow to tiny little slits. Placing her hands on her hips, she cocks her head to one side. Her mouth is creased into a frown.

"What...do...you...want?" she spits at me.

"That's no way to treat a person!" I shout back.

"Because you're *so* special." She looks me up and down. "Aren't you? You're a worthless, untouchable child. Either get what you want or leave."

"A small bag of soap nuts," I shout, "and that's it!" The storekeeper slaps the bag onto an empty spot on the cart and motions for me to place my money on the counter as well. I throw it at her face instead. She screams, and people look at me with disgust. I quickly rush out of town with my bag and pails, distancing myself as much as possible from the horrible people.

The river is close to the edge of the forest. It takes a long time to get there, almost half a day to go back and forth. The sun burns my back, my flimsy sandals offer hardly any protection from the rocks and stones and my arms feel like they're a million pounds from carrying the pails.

At last, I reach the river. No one washes their clothes and dishes in this river, which is why I like it. There's no one to bother me while I do my work. The sparkling water lures me in, telling me to jump in. The sun is burning my back and sweat runs in rivers down my hot, grimy face. *Just one minute...* I think, then shake my head, disgusted with myself. How could I? My family is working hard and I want to play around in the water? No. I begin with the clothes.

I sit on the pebbly beach next to my favorite rock. It's dark gray and completely flat. Not too rough, just right, and big enough to lay out many clothes at a time.

I empty the pail containing the clothes. I fill the empty pail with water and soak the soap nuts in the water. I dunk one of my old blouses into the pail and wring it out. Laying it flat on the rock, I rub the blouse, squeezing the water out of it. Then I dunk it into the river again and again, rubbing all the soap away, wringing it out one last time.

I used to set the clothes out on the grass to let them dry, but the dirt would stick to them and make them soiled again. A few months ago, I found a long piece of twine and tied it to two trees near the water. It worked marvelously to dry the clothes and keep them free of dirt.

I hang my freshly washed blouse on the line and finish washing the rest of the clothes.

Next, I work on the dishes. I dip the coconut rind I brought in the ashes and scrub the dishes with the rind. I rinse all the dishes and dry them with a rag. Then I wash the pail and put the dishes back in the pail.

I check to see if the clothes are dry from the hot sun. They're still damp, so I dip my toes in the cool water and look up at the clouds, at the puffy shapes and figures wafting in the sky. I close my eyes for a moment and imagine I'm high above the river, floating on soft clouds that form pillows underneath me.

A bird chirps and I'm pulled back to reality. Returning my attention to the clothes, I gather them all up off the line and fold them neatly into the pail.

I look up at the sky and realize I've finished early.

I peer at my reflection in the water. Soft, black curls frame my face, large dark brown eyes look like little saucers in the water. My copper-colored skin glistens in the sunlight. With one last glance at her, I dunk my head in the water, feeling the chill course through my bones, refreshing me. Then I make my way back home.

<u>Chapter 4</u>

It feels like ages before I finally see a speck in the distance: home. My body is covered in a thick film of sweat as I slowly walk towards the house. I see Ma outside of the entrance to our house, waving towards me. I reach her, place the pails inside our house, and turn to her.

"Navi, beta, thank you for helping me so much," Ma whispers gratefully, caressing my cheek.

"It's nothing," I say, turning away from her, but she grabs my chin between her thumb and forefinger.

"You deserve more than what I'm able to give you, Navi," she starts. "If I could, I would give you a house made of gold. But I can't. So I was thinking; I could give all the money we got yesterday to you, and –".

"No. No, no, no. We should save it for emergencies," I say, shaking my head and walking away from her. I walk into the washroom with a clean set of clothes and a pail of water and close the curtain.

A few minutes later, I peek from behind the cloth and see that Ma is staring at the curtain. Her expression is sullen and she's looking at the floor. Her eyes are full of sadness and her mouth is pursed into a frown. I can tell she thinks she's failed me again. I shake my head and take my bath. As soon as I'm done bathing in the cold water, I put on fresh clothes and head to my bed to rest for a while.

I take the quilt from Ma's bed and tuck myself in. I look at the ceiling and listen to the twittering of birds outside. I close my eyes, thinking about Papa and how he was always so cheerful and happy. Thinking about Papa's smile, other beautiful memories with him come to my mind. I get out an old sheet of paper and a piece of charcoal. I think of my old house and sketch the big windows and spacious porch. I keep drawing until my artwork is finished, not realizing that a half hour has passed.

The scent of the spicy chicken Ma's making wafts into my nostrils and I smile as she cooks. Rohit isn't inside, and Ma is busy preparing our meal. Suddenly, I hear the clacking of horse hooves outside. Ma pauses for a minute, also hearing the sound of hooves, shrugs and continues stirring her *curry.* The sound comes closer.

"Navi, can you go see what's going on? Rohit is out buying some food and I have to cook," Ma asks.

"Okay," I say, smoothing out my blouse. I put my hair into a quick braid and tie it with a piece of cloth. I pat my langa down, trying to smooth out the wrinkles, and walk outside. I can see a horse approaching and I expect it to go right by our shack or into the forest. I sit down, pluck some blades of grass and braid it.

To my surprise, the horse stops right next to me. I look up, staring at its brilliant black mane and shiny hazelnut coat. The man riding it clears his throat. I look up at him in his dark blue outfit. He has a cloth bag tied around his waist. He looks at the shack, then at me, then back at the shack.

"Are you...Ram's family?" the man asks quizzically. "The guard who committed a sin and then faced –," he continues to ask, his back straight, eyes searing into my skull.

"Yes," I interrupt, "and what would you like?" I stare at him deadpan.

"I have a package for you. Although I don't

understand who would want to send…" he trails off, holding out the package.

"You talk too much," I say in a steely voice and snatch the package from his outstretched hand. "You should leave."

He pulls on the reigns and turns his beautiful horse around. He shoots me a nasty glare before galloping away. I watch until he becomes a speck in the distance and then retreat back into our house. Ma is setting up the bowls on the mat. She glances over, patting a spot next to her.

"Come. What was that about?" she asks curiously.

"We got a package," I reply flatly.

I sit down next to her and set the package down between us. Rohit finally returns with some food for tomorrow's meal and joins us.

"Did something happen while I was gone?" he asks, sensing the tension in the air.

"We got another package," I reply. His face lights up at the news.

"Can we open it?" he exclaims, his eyes lighting up.

"We can, but let's eat first," Ma replies.

For dinner, we each have two small pieces of spiced chicken and three chunks of boiled potato with one small *roti*. On the side, as a treat, we each have one piece of tamarind that Rohit foraged that morning.

Unlike Rohit, who gobbles all of his food up, I chew mine slowly, savoring it.

After we've all finished, we stare at the package, waiting for someone to break the silence.

"So...should we open it?" Rohit slowly asks. Ma nods her head, also eagerly waiting.

"Ok," I say. I start to open the package and a letter slides out. Rohit and Ma huddle behind me, reading the letter over my shoulder.

Dear Friends,

It's me again. You're probably wondering who I really am. I'm so sorry I can't give you a formal introduction. If anyone sees this letter, I will be in big trouble. That is why I can't give you my name. I can only say that I am part of the royal family.

Last time I gave you coins. That will help you for a little while, but the time will come when you spend the last coin.

Then your life will be back to normal, back to the same old problems. I promised Ram that I would help his family, and giving you coins is not going to be enough. Thus, I have formed a plan.

It may sound crazy, but you should just leave. Run far away from this nasty place.

I paused. This person, from the royal family, was calling their own kingdom a nasty place? I continue reading, more perplexed than ever.

I know a way out of the kingdom so you can leave this place. It will take you to the next kingdom, Amarender's Kingdom. The path is through the Kushan Forest. Every now and then, you will also see bright pink flowers growing along the way, signaling you are on the right path.

When you reach the end of the path, you will meet a friend of mine, Aditi, in a shack the size of yours. It is bright red, so you should spot it right away. Aditi is part of the royal family in Amarender's Kingdom. She will give you some fancy clothes to wear. She will introduce you to her papa, the king, as friends who she met many years ago. Then she will find you a nice place to stay and find jobs.

I know this is just a temporary plan for your stay away from here, but I will figure the rest out with Aditi. If you would like to go, you must leave just before dawn tomorrow. It will take about two days to get there, if you rest at night. She will be waiting for you when you arrive.

You don't have to go through with the plan. I know this is a lot to take in, and you may not want to risk the journey. But if you do, I will do whatever I can to help you get away from here. It's your choice. If you follow through with the plan, I wish you a good journey!

Sincerely,
A friend

Chapter 5

I read the letter over and over again, shock and confusion filling me. I glance at Ma and Rohit and see that they look shocked, too. A hundred questions fill my head.

Ma and Rohit finally pull away from the letter. There is silence between us for a while and all we can hear is the sound of crickets singing outside.

"We should do it." Rohit's voice cuts through the silence like a knife, sharp and quick.

I look at him.

"But should we Rohit?" I ask. "Think logically. Do you really think that this plan will work? The letter said it's only temporary. What if we can't figure out a permanent plan? Will we keep running for the rest of lives?"

"Well, would you rather live this wonderful life?" He says, sarcastically.

"It's not just that, Rohit."

"Well, what is it then? What's stopping us?"

"Rohit —" Ma tries to cut in.

"Well think about it, Rohit —" I start.

"This should be an easy decision —" Rohit cuts in.

"STOP!" Ma commands.

We both turn to her.

"You are both right. There are pros and cons about leaving. But the thing is, there are three people here. So it's a voting matter, and I do have an opinion," Ma states. "Navi, you are correct. Maybe we should be scared and not trust this person. And there are other reasons we shouldn't go."

She looks at me while she says this. She knows me too well.

"But I have to say, Rohit is correct, too. This life is tiring us. You aren't having the life that a child should have. You act like adults. You are wearing yourselves out. And the worst part is that I see you suffering each day…" Ma's eyes glisten with tears.

"I see you work too hard for your age. I see you come home beaten and hurt, and I don't even know how or what happened. By bullies? By people who hate Papa?" She looks right at me when she says that. "It's not just that. You stay hungry day and night, and I can't do a thing about it. I go to bed at night, feeling guilty that my children can't even have a full stomach." She pauses for a while, tears cascading down her beautiful cheeks.

"I love both of you the most in the world. You are my life. When you suffer every day, it feels like someone has stabbed me in the heart." Rohit rushes to her side and hugs her.

"If there was just one night where your stomach was full, and you weren't covered in bruises, it would mean the world to me. I would do anything for it." She smiles a little at the thought. "And wouldn't you want a new life, too? Wouldn't you?" she says, locking eyes with me.

"So I say we leave," she states firmly. I stare at her for a long time. The room is dead silent.

"Ma...you mean the world to me, too...so I will do as you say," I tell her. I start to walk out of the shack, but Ma stops me. She pulls me in, hugs me tightly and whispers in my ear, "I love you, Navi. I love you more than anything. For once, I can actually do something to help you, beta. I really, really want this for you and Rohit. It will be a fresh start."

"I know," I say, pulling away from her embrace. "But maybe we don't need a fresh start."

"I know you don't want to leave. But isn't it better to just start over with a new life?" Ma says.

She looks into my eyes, both her hands on my shoulders. I look away from her gaze. "I guess you're right," I finally manage.

Ma sighs. "One day, you will understand, Navi, but now it's time to sleep. We all need our rest for tomorrow. It's going to be a big day." Her eyes are bright and she's smiling.

"You should sleep. I'll be outside for a few minutes," I say.

"Ok. Come in after a few minutes. I love you." Ma climbs into bed and falls asleep immediately.

Outside, I sit down, leaning on our shack to look at the scenery. It's beautiful. I never noticed it before. The sun is setting, coloring the sky with yellow and orange hues and illuminating the clouds bright pink. The tops of trees are painted a golden yellow, and small blue butterflies fly around them. Eagles swirl high in the sky and crickets chirp in the fresh green grass, which is glowing gold like raisins. The gravel road looks like a bronze gateway to the prettiest, most perfect land. But it's all an illusion.

After a while, the sky turns a dark royal blue with twinkling little stars. A full moon lights up the sky, casting the road in a white glow.

"I couldn't fall asleep," Rohit says, startling me. I look up at him and then back at the beautiful landscape.

"It's beautiful, isn't it?" I murmur.

"I bet it'll be prettier when you're watching from a palace terrace." He grins.

"Ya, right," I say.

"Navya, why is this so hard for you? Don't you want a fresh start? I thought you were the brave one." I sigh and look up at him.

I choose my words carefully. "This is not brave, Rohit. This is cowardly. We're running away from problems that many others have to face every day. I do want a new life, but not just for us. I want a new life for every untouchable. I'm not scared about leaving, Rohit. I just think it's wrong. That's why I don't want to do it. It's wrong. The caste system is wrong. It's all wrong," I say.

He looks down at me. "I know you care about others, and I know you think leaving is wrong. But the only way to actually help people like us is to get to a higher caste and make people understand what it's like to be the lowest. So yes, we need to do this even though it might feel selfish right now. It will allow us to do good, in the long term."

I consider his case. After a long pause, I say, "I guess you're right."

"I am, Navi," he replies softly. He walks back into the shack as I stare into the sky and finally drift asleep under the stars.

Chapter 6

I awake to the sun's bright glare in my eyes and blink a few times as my eyes adjust to the light. I go inside and find Ma bustling about the shack with a big smile on her face.

"Where's Rohit?" I grumble.

"He went to the forest to get some more fruit for the journey." Ma glides around the room, collecting things she needs in a small bag.

"Oh," I say. Ma looks over at me and pauses.

"Navi, can you please be in a good mood?" Ma pleads with me.

"I'm fine," I say unconvincingly.

She turns away and looks at the portrait of Papa. She touches it gingerly and stares at his face longingly. "I wish we could take this with us," Ma sighs.

I go outside as Rohit runs towards me, his basket full of colorful fruit. "What are you going to take with you?" I ask.

"What?" he says, blinking.

"I mean, to take when we leave," I clarify.

"I haven't decided if I want to remember this place or forget it," he says, scratching his nose.

We walk back into the shack and I walk over to my bed. My mother hands me a bag to put my stuff in. I stuff my blanket and quilt from my bed, then gingerly pull the coins from the straw and add them to the bottom of the bag. I place my special paint brush on top and look around, trying to think of what else to bring. Then I remember.

"Here. Now you will never forget me. I love you, Navi."

Papa told me that before he left us. A tear trickles down my face, but I quickly swipe it away. I move my straw bed aside and look at the dirt ground underneath it. In one spot, instead of dirt, I'd dug a hole and covered it with stones. Setting the stones aside, I pluck the small sack from the hole and remove the hat and gold chain that Papa had given me before he left.

I clasp the chain around my neck and brush the dust off the hat to inspect it. It's dark blue with a black velvet top and a gold patch on the front. Carefully, I place it in my pack and tie it shut with a piece of string.

Sitting on the ground, the pack held tightly in my hand, I let tears fall to the ground, leaving drops of salty water on the earth. My mind drifts to Papa on that day, and what he said:

"I'll never leave you, Navi. Ever. I'll always be here. In there," he says, pointing to my heart. "I will help you when you are in need, and I will show you the right paths to take, dear. I'll never leave your side. I promise you that."

I put my arms around my knees and squeeze as hard as I can and curl into a tiny ball. For a moment, I can feel his tight embrace. *Why did you have to leave me, Papa?* I wonder as I hug my knees to my chest and weep softly.

"Are you ready?" Rohit whispers softly in my ear.

I nod my head. "Yes."

"It'll be good. You'll like it, Navi," Rohit assures me.

"Hmm," I murmur.

"What?" he asks.

"Maybe I'll like it," I say, not at all convinced. I walk out of the shack following Ma and Rohit. He smiles, happy he finally got to me.

I stop and look around, soaking up everything that I'll be leaving behind. The fresh, sweet scent of the air right after it rains. The sopping trees around our shack, next to the forest. The butterflies fluttering to and fro. The muddy puddles. The sky full of white, puffy clouds you could get lost daydreaming in. Everything here, it must be the definition of prettiness. The meaning of beauty.

Rohit nudges me. "Everything will work out, right?" I ask him.

"Right," he answers.

"And when we finally get there, I can help people like us?" I ask uncertainly.

"Right," he confirms. Ma waits for us by the edge of the forest. She waves and smiles, motioning for us to join her. We walk towards her and her eagerness is palpable. When we reach her, she starts walking deeper into the forest. Rohit and I follow, a few steps behind. My family is happy. I start to have a glimmer of hope. Maybe I have a bright future ahead of me. I can help others like me.

"Rohit?" I ask.

"Ya?" he answers.

"I've changed my mind. I'll like it for sure," I say assuredly.

"Really? I mean, you never give up easily," he says, looking at me out of the corner of his eye.

After a moment of thought, I continue. "I thought about what you said last night. It is frustrating that I can't make a change by being an untouchable, but it is reality. No one will ever listen to me as I am now. If I can ascend to a higher caste, then maybe people will listen to me. Maybe I can free the lower castes from their misery by making people understand how awful it is. Maybe I can make a change and free everyone from their castes. After all, the only thing the caste system does is prevent people from reaching their dreams, from reaching their full potential."

Maybe this won't be so bad after all.

Chapter 7

We walk, and walk, and walk. So much walking. And as our friend said, there are bright pink flowers along the path every now and then.

After a while, Ma makes us stop near one of the flowering bushes. We sit down to rest and Ma takes out a few mangoes from her bag and hands us the bright orange fruits.

"Here's your breakfast." Ma smiles.

I finish my mango, enjoying the pops of flavor in my mouth. The chewiness, the sweetness, the slightly sour tinge. After I finish, I go over to the flowering bush nearby. It has wonderful deep orangey-pink flowers. The center is a dark purple, which accents the orange. They're surrounded by dark, thick green leaves.

I pluck a few of the small flowers and walk over to Ma. Her black curls are pulled into a thick braid. I tuck the flowers into the braid, making sure they won't fall out. She laughs as we get up to continue our journey.

The forest is beautiful. It's full of luscious plants. The sunlight peaks through many layers of leaves, casting a golden glow onto the ground. The shafts of sunlight keep the forest well lit, yet mysterious at the same time.

The sun starts to set and an orangey-pink light envelopes the forest. We find a good place to rest in the crook of two trees. It creates a bed-like corner filled with leaves to soften the hard ground. It is also high enough so we can look out for wild animals. I hear a creek nearby, and realize we won't have to worry about water. Slivers of light shine from above. I open my pack and put my blanket down so it covers the whole area. We all sit down on it.

"I was just thinking about that time," Ma starts. "You were young. Papa and I got up, and we couldn't find you. We looked everywhere and woke up Rohit too, asking if he had seen you. He said he didn't."

"Oh, I remember that!" he laughs, recalling the memory. "So we went outside to ask our neighbors if they had seen you," Rohit adds. "And you were sitting there right in front of us, playing in a puddle of muddy water. It was raining and you were having the time of your life."

They laugh, reminiscing, and I join in.

"You were a naughty kid," Ma says.

"I'm not surprised," I answer, winking at her.

"I think we should sleep now, get well rested for tomorrow," Ma says.

"Ok," I agree.

I wrap myself in my quilt and peer up at the deep night sky twinkling with stars. I close my eyes and envision the fancy clothes Aditi will have for me to wear when we get out of the forest.

Maybe it's an orange langa covered in silk embroidery, I wonder. *Or maybe a green ghagra with a beautiful gold and pink border. Gold jewelry studded with diamonds and emeralds and rubies... Whatever it is, I bet it will be beautiful.*

I wake up early and see that both Ma and Rohit are sleeping peacefully. Fragments of pale blue light shine from above. I reach into my pack and pluck out my paintbrush. Looking around to see if I can find any berries to make pigments, I meander around, collecting little things: bright flowers, deep berries, fragrant spices. I peel a thin layer of bark from a tree to paint on and head back to Rohit and

Ma to find them still sound asleep. I sit down next to them and get to work.

I smooth the piece of bark out, dust it off and close my eyes, remembering the night before we left the shack as I crush various berries to make pigments of color. I imagine the golden treetops and the orange sky and begin to paint. Using the tip of my finger to blend colors, I work intently, with purpose. Finally, I add a bit of blue to complete the last butterfly and step back to inspect my finished work.

It's not bad, I decide, but it's not alive. I grab a handful of the wet dirt beneath me and grind it up. Then I mix a tiny bit of the dirt into a shiny yellow color, creating a subdued, burnt yellow with a gritty texture and tone. I sweep it across the road in my painting. Much better.

At last, Ma wakes up. She comes over and looks at my work. "Navi, it's beautiful," she whispers in awe.

"It's not bad," I reply.

"Papa was an artist too, you know," she says softly.

"I know," I respond, feeling that familiar lump in my throat.

"One day, you'll be as good as him," Ma says.

"I hope so," I manage.

She walks over to a nearby tree and plucks a big green leaf from one of its sturdy branches. She folds it into a cup shape and scoops the crisp, cold water from the creek into it, gulping it down. It's quiet except for the sound of a few birds chirping in the distance. I close my eyes, soaking in the sounds of life. I stay like that, absorbed in the sound of nature. But then I hear another sound. A creaking sound. I open my eyes as Ma turns to look at me at the same time. It wasn't just me who heard it. There's another sound, the sound of horse hooves stomping the ground. It comes closer, then stops abruptly.

Rohit wakes up and sees our startled expressions. He opens his mouth to say something, but I press a finger to my mouth, shushing him.

"Don't move," Ma mouths to us. The birds have stopped singing. The forest is eerily still, silent.

And then I hear a scream.

Chapter 8

The sound of horse hooves start again, but this time, they move further and further away. When we can't hear them any longer, I run towards the scream. Ma and Rohit chase after me, trying to stop me.

"What are you doing, Navya? Come back this instant!" Ma shouts at me.

"Navya, come back! You don't know what's out there!" Rohit screams.

I ignore them and finally stop at the edge of a deep gorge in the middle of the forest. It cascades down from all sides and looks like the mouth of a hungry giant eating up the forest. I see a figure at the bottom, covered in mud with an arrow at his side.

"Help," he pleads, looking up at us.

"Hang on, sir. I'll help you. You don't have to worry. You're going to be ok," I assure the man.

His hair covers his face, which I can see is plastered with dirt. Ma and Rohit finally catch up and stop by me, panting.

"How are we going to get him?" Rohit asks me, trying to catch his breath.

I circle around the edge and find an easy way to descend. I climb down, inching to the man's side. I see that he has a deep gash on his leg and an arrow sticking out of his side. As I reach for him, he pulls back.

"It's ok, sir. I'm not going to hurt you," I tell the man. "I'm just going to help you walk up and bring you to my family up there, alright?"

I point over to Ma and Rohit, who look shocked and worried. I help him up and throw his arm around my shoulder. Very slowly, I inch back towards Ma and Rohit. By the time I'm up the hill, I'm sweating and out of breath.

"Let's go back to our spot," Ma says.

"It will take too much time," Rohit replies.

"It's our only choice. This man is hurt and my medicine is back there," she says. I've already started walking, struggling not to buckle under his weight. Rohit rushes towards me and props his other arm around his shoulders to help carry him.

We finally get to our spot and set him down next to the blanket we slept on last night. He is panting and weak. Ma rushes over to examine the wound on his right side. I sit across from him as Ma goes to work.

"This might hurt," she warns. With one swift move, she pulls the arrow out. The man grunts in pain. Ma asks us to clean the wound. Rohit and I walk the man to the creek and splash water onto the wound as he winces. Ma brings him back to the tree and puts some medicine on the wound. Removing a piece of clean cloth from her bag, she carefully places it on the wound and wraps it around his body to form a bandage.

He leans against the tree, exhausted. "Thank you," he whispers, his eyes closed.

Ma nods. The man turns to me and looks me in the eyes.

"Do I know you? You look familiar," he says slowly.

"I'm sorry, sir, I don't think so," I reply.

He closes his eyes. "It's been a long day. I think I'd like some sleep," he says. Ma nods her head, even though he can't see her. He falls asleep a minute after closing his eyes. I stand there, staring at his face. I search his face, trying to figure out if I know him, but it's covered in a veil of dirt. I hadn't paid attention to how he looked when I rescued him.

"I wonder what happened to this poor man," Ma says. She trembles and her eyes are big and shiny. I get up and hug her.

"It's ok, Ma. He'll be ok. Let us give him some time to rest," I suggest. She nods in agreement and heads down to the creek. She sits on a flat rock and rests her head against a tree. I can tell she is worried. I am worried, too. Finding this man is a complication we do not need.

"I bet he's rich," Rohit says matter-of-factly.

"What?" I whip my head around to look at Rohit, who is sitting next to me, by the man.

"Look. He has a bunch of gold rings on his fingers with different stones. See? That one has a diamond and that one has an emerald," he tells me, pointing at them.

"Why does it matter?" I ask nonchalantly.

"It was just an observation," Rohit shrugs. I look at his hands, each finger displaying a ring. Then I look at his clothes. Though they are ripped from his fall, they are nice clothes. Very nice.

"Hey, look at that one! It looks really familiar," Rohit says, pointing to a gold ring with an oval-shaped ruby embedded in it.

"It does!" I gasp. *Who have I seen wearing a ring like that?* I wonder.

"Or maybe he's not rich at all. Maybe he's a thief. He was obviously running from someone," Rohit says.

"Why do you think so?" I ask.

"Well we heard the sound of horse hooves. Someone must have been chasing him on the horses, and then the person shot him with the arrow," he explains.

"It's possible," I reply slowly. We sit in silence for a long time. I go to the creek and splash water on my face. I begin to feel anxious, wondering if we'll be able to continue with the journey. Ma starts a small fire and takes some vegetables out of her bag to cook.

After what seems like forever, the man wakes up. We look at him, wondering if he'll tell us who he is.

He ignores us for the moment and gets up slowly. I can see the rusty color of dried blood around his wound. He's clearly in a lot of pain. I wonder if he can even stand up. I step forward to help, but he raises a hand.

"I'm just going to the creek to clean up," he says. He limps to the creek and splashes water onto his face, washing the dirt away. My heart starts beating fast, but I can't figure out why. *He's just washing his face, Navya,* I think. *Calm down.*

When he turns to look at us, Rohit and I collectively gasp. Ma's smile disappears when she realizes who it is. My surprise quickly turns into anger.

He has a glint in his hazel-brown eyes and his black hair skims his shoulders. He has a tight smile on his face, full of ego.

"You-you're –," Rohit starts.

"The king. Dayananda," Ma finishes.

Chapter 9

"Yes. I am Dayananda the King," he bellows, "and you are?"

My hands are clenched at my sides, blood rushing to my face. "I look familiar, huh?" I yell at him.

"Why yes, I did say that, but there's no reason to yell at me," he says, clearly annoyed.

"Stop, Navi," Ma whispers.

"What's going on?" He demands, looking back and forth between each of us.

"You have no clue, do you?" I spit at him, "Maybe I look like my father, Ram."

"There are many people named 'Ram' who I know. You'll have to be more specific," he says.

"He was a guard. Until you killed him!" I shout.

Rohit comes up behind me and puts a hand on my shoulder. "Navi," he says, trying to calm me down

I shrug his hand off my shoulder. "You know. The

one from the fire? The fire that burned half your palace? He saved an untouchable and the queen's sister, Aishani?" I ask.

"Oh, yes. Him." Dayananda's says dismissively. I look up at him with pure hatred in my eyes.

"Well, what can I say? The rules are you have to save members of the royal family and brahmins before anyone else. And did he really have to save an untouchable? They're worthless. He deserved what he got," he says dismissively.

It takes all of the self-restraint I have to not lunge and throw myself at the king standing before me. "Oh really? And guess what? The people who just saved you," I point to myself, Rohit and Ma, "are untouchables. So yes, I guess you're right. Untouchables *are* worthless, aren't they? What good is it to save you?" I lock eyes with the king.

"Navya…" Ma says feebly.

"What?" I ask without looking at her, my eyes fixed on the king's.

Ma turns to Dayananda. "Please, sit down. Navya, can I talk to you?" She steers me away from him with a firm hand and stops after we are well out of his hearing range.

"Navi, please. Calm down," Ma says.

"It's dangerous being with him. Let's leave. Let's continue our journey. This is all the more reason to escape. If he figures out what we are planning, then he will punish us, maybe even kill us," I whisper, trying to convince my mother.

"He's hurt. He has lost too much blood. He won't survive if we leave him here. We need to help him," she says.

"No! No. We already treated his wound. You saw him! He was able to walk just fine. We should leave and meet Aditi on the other side of this forest," I protest.

"What would you do if it was someone else?" Ma asks me.

"What do you mean?" I say, unsure of what she's getting at.

"If it was someone else, would you help him?"

"Yes, but –"

"It doesn't matter who it is. You should help someone no matter who they are; isn't that right? If Papa was here, do you know what he would want you to do?" she asks softly, her eyes damp.

After a few moments, I sigh and say, "He'd want me to help the person."

"Exactly. We will give him all the help we can offer. Because that's the kind of people we are. Do you understand?" she asks, looking at me intently.

"Yes," I say reluctantly.

"Thank you," Ma sighs as she holds my chin in her hand and kisses my forehead. Then she goes back to preparing dinner. *How can she do that, just act like everything's normal and the man right next to her didn't kill Papa?* I ponder disbelievingly.

I sit down next to her and cross my arms. She serves the food into three bowls and hands one to me, one to Rohit and one to Dayananda.

"What about you?" I say.

"I'm fine," Ma says.

I watch Dayananda bring a piece of food to his mouth and crinkle his nose. He chews through it slowly. I clench my fists at my sides. *Poor him,* I stew bitterly. *It's not good enough for his high taste.*

I push my bowl towards Ma. "I've lost my appetite," I say, staring at the king. Ma opens her mouth, but I jump up and run away.

"Let her be. She needs time to herself," Rohit whispers to Ma.

I run for a long, long time. When I can't run any longer and my legs are about to give out, I stop and put my hands on my knees, panting.

Well, you better say goodbye to your pretty dresses, I decide. I pick up a rock and throw it at the nearest tree. Leaning against another tall tree, I close my eyes and suck in a series of long, deep breaths. Slowly, I turn to walk back towards the group. By the time I return, Rohit and Ma are fast asleep. Dayananda is awake, staring into the burning fire. I sit across from him, staring into the dancing flames. The wood slowly burns, creating orange embers that turn black and charred. When the wind blows the right – or wrong – way, the air is filled with thick smoke. I peer up through the layers of thick leaves up high and see the dark sky sprinkled with bright white twinkling stars and wish more than anything at that moment that I could fly.

I've almost forgotten I'm not alone, until Dayananda breaks the silence. "Your family deserves a handsome reward for saving me. I'm thinking lots of gold," he says.

I stare at him incredulously, his eyes glowing orange from the flames, and wonder if he's serious.

"To start off, here's one of my rings," he says. He hands me the huge ring embedded with the ruby. I run my fingers over it.

"You're serious," I laugh bitterly, and throw the ring back at him, "I don't need or want your gold."

I turn away from the fire to walk away, but he yells after me.

"Well then what do you want? I can buy you anything! I can get you anything!" he exclaims.

"Oh really?" I say, mocking him. I walk back to the fire and stop about a foot away from him.

"Can you buy me my father, Dayananda? Can you buy me a better life? Can you buy all the untouchables better lives? If you can, let me know," I spew.

"You know I can't give you that," he says.

"Of course you can't give me that! All you care about are your ridiculous rules. The untouchables don't deserve the lives they have. Castes do nothing but label people. I know nobody will ever do anything about it but, I wanted to make a difference. I wanted to change how people think. I wanted to free people from their castes, but it looks like you stole that chance away from me by showing up here. You take away everything I care about, don't you?" I say, my shrill voice cutting the night like a knife. Tears spring up into my eyes.

I walk over to where Rohit and Ma are sleeping and sit down as the king sits, speechless. I throw my quilt at him.

"You're probably used to nice, soft mattresses. Sorry we don't have a big supply of those. You can use my blanket. Goodnight," I snarl. And with that, I curl up into a ball and fall into a restless sleep.

Chapter 10

I wake up before everyone else and walk to the creek to splash some water on my face and hands. I spend some time cleaning up all the dirt and grit from the previous day. It invigorates me a little. I splash water on my sandals and set them out to dry. Turning around, I grumble. Dayananda is sitting down on the ground, inspecting my painting.

"Did you paint this? It's really good," he murmurs.

"Yes," I answer flatly.

"Is that where you live, that small shack thing? It's so tiny, and –" he starts.

"Yes," I say a little louder this time.

He stops talking and studies the painting. I notice that my pack is open wide, as if someone scrambled for something inside. "Were you trying to look for something?" I ask him.

He doesn't answer.

"Why is my pack wide open?" I ask, getting irritated.

"Are you questioning the king?" he says angrily.

"You can't just go through someone's stuff. And anyways, what could I possibly have that is of interest to you?" I demand.

He doesn't answer. I walk barefoot on the prickly grass, kissed with small balls of dew, and kneel by my bag. It looks messed up; everything is tossed around. I see my father's hat, the insignia glinting in the early morning light. It looks as if it had been dusted off, thoroughly cleaned even.

"Did you wash the hat? Please tell me you didn't," I say.

"No, I just dusted it off. It was grimy. Why is it so important anyways?" he says, acting annoyed.

I can't believe his ridiculous attitude.

"You don't have any right to rummage through my stuff. And what do you know about me? Nothing. I don't need to tell you, but I will anyways. It was my father's. The last thing he gave to me before he…before he left," I state.

"I don't care," Dayananda says carelessly.

"And I don't care about you, either. If it were up to me, I'd leave you here. By the way, why are you even here, your Highness?" I say, crossing my arms.

"I don't need to do any explaining. I'm the king," he retorts.

"Well if you want our help, you've got to tell us something, don't you? The forest isn't going to bow to your feet, sir," I say.

Hearing all the commotion, Ma and Rohit wake up and come over.

"Good morning," I say with a tight smile.

"How are you feeling?" Ma asks me.

"Oh just wonderful. What is the plan for this lovely day?" I say sarcastically.

Ma ignores my comment and turns to Dayananda.

"How is your pain? I should have another look at the bandage. Please sit down," she says.

Dayananda sits down next to the charred remains of the fire. Ma sits down next to him and carefully examines the bandage. She applies some more medicine to his leg, which looks pretty bad.

Dayananda winces and Ma looks up at his face. "Who was following you? And why did they shoot you?" she asks him.

Straightening, Dayananda explains, "I was out hunting with my bodyguard when some enemy soldiers circled us. We were outnumbered. I sent my bodyguard to warn my generals and put the palace under lockdown. I ran and tried to escape, but they shot me with that arrow. Figuring that I was dead, they left. Now I have to get back to the palace, but first, I need to make sure it is safe to return. I need somewhere to stay for a day or two until I figure things out."

As he finishes his story, we all quietly mull it over. Then Ma says something I do not expect.

"If you wanted, you could stay in our house for a day. It's not...it's not much, but it will do. It is at the edge of the forest, safe from prying eyes. We could start heading back right now if you want," Ma replies.

Dayananda ponders the offer. "I never imagined stepping into an untouchable's house, but I guess I'll have to deal with it," Dayananda says. I feel my blood beginning to boil. I am about to say something when he asks, "What are you guys doing out in this forest anyway?"

I sigh and close my eyes, rubbing my forehead. *Why couldn't we just have left before this question was asked?* I plead silently, looking at Ma.

"We were escaping from your wretched kingdom. Someone from the royal family sent us letters to help us get to the next kingdom where we wouldn't be untouchables anymore. But then you came," I announce matter-of-factly.

Dayananda's jaw drops and he looks shocked. I smile at him slyly.

"That's...that..." he stutters.

"What are you going to do about it? Kill us after we've saved your life and given you a place to stay? Just like when you killed my father for saving another man's life?" I taunt.

"Navi, stop!" Ma says, trying to shush me.

I hold my tongue and glare at Dayananda. Streaks of pale sunlight illuminate his face. Maybe it's the way the light falls on his face, but for the first time, I see a flash of doubt on his face.

Rohit clears his throat, breaking the silence. "Let's start heading back," he says.

I nod and pull my damp sandals on. I tie my pack up and throw it over my shoulder. Dayananda gets up and gingerly puts weight on his leg. He takes a few painful steps, but then sees the painting and stops. He bends and picks it up.

"Keep it," I tell him.

We start our long walk back, Rohit helping the king along the way.

"I just don't understand. Why wouldn't you want all my gifts? I could buy you anything you want and you refuse. Why?" Dayananda asks, shaking his head in disbelief.

"Buying me stuff isn't going to erase the pain I have faced in the last four years. And I don't want anything. I don't care for material objects," I say.

"That's odd," Dayananda says.

"Maybe to you it is. The only thing you find joy in is gold," I say.

Dayananda mumbles to himself, but doesn't reply. As we continue our journey, I think about what the future might bring.

Chapter 11

The next day, we reach our old shack. I sense Dayananda's hesitation as he steps inside. He looks around and then sits down in our old chair.

Ma immediately starts giving us jobs to do around the house now that we have a guest. As I tidy up the sleeping area, I glance at Papa's portrait. Dayananda stands next to it, looking into Papa's eyes, which are full of life and love. Rohit and Ma bustle around, tidying up the other areas for the new guest.

Dayananda has a funny look on his face. I can't tell if it's regret, or remorse, or something else. He turns away from the portrait and inspects our shack curiously. I look away before he can see me looking at him and place the contents of my pack into the small hole under my bed.

Ma heats up a pail of water we filled before we left – our only water. She places it behind the curtain.

"You can take a shower," she calls to Dayananda.

Our only water. And then she does something

unbelievable. She hands him the only pair of Papa's clothes that we have, the ones we took before leaving our old house. She hands them to Dayananda. Papa's only clothes that we own.

Dayananda goes into the bathroom and Ma walks up to me. "Can you go check if any stores are open? They might not be because of the lockdown," Ma says. She hands me a few coins. I finger them, the metal cold against my hot skin.

"If they are open, get some vegetables and chicken. I'll make some dinner," she says.

"Ok," I sigh, heading out of the house.

The clouds hang low against a dull gray sky as I walk to the center of town. The marketplace is empty, giving it an eerie, deserted look. A crow scurries past me with a few stale crumbs in its mouth. I turn and head back home.

"They were all closed," I tell Ma when I return.

"We'll have to look for vegetables in the garden then," she says, sighing.

"We don't have to have dinner, Ma. We aren't hungry," I lie.

"We are hosting the king, Navi. We have to give

him food," she whispers.

"He doesn't even enjoy your meals!" I yell.

She stares at me, her mouth slightly agape, looking stunned. "I'm sorry, but –" I start.

"You know what, Navi? You have to learn to be kind," she snaps and walks out of the house to find vegetables. Now it's my turn to be stunned. I sit down on my bed and pull Papa's hat out of my pack, thinking about Dayananda.

I try to collect my thoughts, but it's as if I have a devil sitting on one shoulder and an angel on the other. *Ma's right. Hating him isn't going to bring Papa back.*

Ma isn't right! The wretched man killed Papa! How can you let it go?

My head spins as my conflicting thoughts ping back and forth. I set Papa's hat down on my bed and then walk towards Ma, who is cooking dinner.

"Ma…I'm sorry about what I said earlier. I just don't understand how you can stand the man who k-killed Papa. And that's not the only thing! He's also caused us all this misery! We are in this situation, where we can't even afford enough food to have three meals a day. How do you do it? How can you forgive someone so easily?" I say.

Ma stirs the pot of steaming curry with a wooden spoon. Finally, she dips her finger in, tasting the fragrant mixture. Then she looks up at me, deep in thought.

"I see how it must be hard for you to understand how I can tolerate such a man so easily," Ma says. She looks around the counter, finds a container with some spice and puts a dash of it in the curry. Then she says, "I don't fully understand it either."

She stirs the curry for a few more minutes and then sets it aside.

"And?" I ask as she wipes her hands on a rag nearby.

"Why don't we go outside," Ma says, leading me outside the shack into the glowing orange sunlight, out of Dayananda's earshot.

"Ma, are you going to tell me or not?" I ask impatiently.

"Navi, the thing is, the reason I'm helping him is because of Papa. Papa had his strong opinions, but he treated everyone kindly and with respect. And in the forest, believe me, I was angry. But when I thought about it, I realized what Papa would have wanted me to do. Papa would want me to help Dayananda and be kind to him. And when I thought about it more, I realized Dayananda should realize what it is like, to be an untouchable. To see the life we live. Maybe it would show him a different perspective," Ma explains.

We stay silent for a while and then I break the silence. "How would Papa forgive a man who killed him?"

"Papa could find kindness and love in anyone. Even Dayananda. Papa would say, 'Holding a grudge is easy, but what does anger do? Anger doesn't make a change.' Instead, I think Papa would teach Dayananda that the caste system is wrong," Ma says.

I find this hard to understand.

"Think about it, Navi," Ma says.

We head back inside and then Ma sets the bowls down and puts some rice with curry in them. She calls Rohit and Dayananda for dinner. The food seems tasteless. After we finish, Ma takes all our bowls and places them in the dirty dishes pail.

"You can use my bed," I tell Dayananda.

Ma looks at me with a mix of confusion and surprise on her face. I walk outside and listen to the muffled noises going on inside of the shack. The crash of dirty dishes, the padding of feet on the ground, soft voices and finally, the quietness of sleep.

I sit with my back against the wall of the shack, looking up at the sky. The dark blue beckons me and I feel like I'm falling into the vastness of space and stars. Sadly, a voice brings me crashing back down to Earth.

"Couldn't sleep?" Dayananda asks.

"Wasn't trying to," I reply.

I look up and see him looking at the sky, too. His rings glint in the greenish-silver moonlight. We stay like that for a while, both looking at the sky.

"I have a daughter a little older than you," he says, trying to strike conversation.

"Oh," I reply flatly.

"You know, I've always wanted to ask you something," I say.

"Go on," Dayananda says.

"When you saw Papa after the fire and ordered him executed, did he act like he regretted his actions?" I ask.

"I think his only regret was leaving you and your family," Dayananda says.

After a while, Dayananda whispers, "Sometimes, I regret my decisions."

"Really? But I thought you were perfect!" I say, feigning surprise.

"What I'm trying to say is that I've made some mistakes that maybe I shouldn't have," he says as he looks up thoughtfully into the dark trees. A tear slides down my cheek.

"Of course you have!" I scream in my head, but I stay quiet, plucking blades of grass from the dirt.

"Was that an apology?" I ask finally.

He doesn't answer. I look back and see him for a split second as he slips back through the doorway.

Chapter 12

I wake up to sunlight creeping under my eyelids. They flutter open, and I see a handful of grass in my hand. I let it fall to the ground, watching each blade flutter and do a few twirls until it softly touches the ground. I wipe my hands on my langa and head inside. Ma sees me and smiles.

"Navi, can you please take the king for a walk? I just changed his bandages. He is doing much better, but he will need some exercise" Ma says.

"Can you go?" I ask hopefully.

"I would, but someone has to clean up around here," Ma replies. The irritation my request caused her is clear in her voice.

"Fine," I say, going outside to wait. I lean against the shack until Dayananda comes out.

"Let's go," he says.

I start walking on the gravel road and he walks by my side. He looks like a very ordinary person in plain clothes, not at all like a king. We pass many run-down shacks on our walk. Since we live so far away from the palace and no one really cares about us, the lockdown has little effect here. Kids are out doing their daily chores. I watch his face out of the corner of my eye. He looks around, observing all the unfamiliar sights.

"What are you thinking right now? Tell me the truth," I say.

"I'm thinking about how horrible these shacks are. I mean, can't these people even build a proper house? It's not that hard. And look at those children. They are all so filthy. And all of them are playing outside or working. Can't they even try to improve their lives?" he says with disdain.

My hands immediately become fists and I feel my anger bubbling up inside of me. Then I remember what Ma said. I slowly unclench my fists.

"Don't you understand? These people are limited because of their caste. Most of these children can't go to school because they are untouchables. They have to spend their days doing dirty jobs that pay almost nothing. These families live in shacks like that because they can't afford money for houses, and even if they could, they aren't allowed to live near other castes. It's a cycle. If they weren't labeled as untouchables, they could probably do amazing things with their lives, but now their futures are barren," I say.

Dayananda scowls and says, "It is their fate! What can I do?"

"Well, for one, you could start by actually caring," I say.

We keep walking. I see a young girl sweeping the streets.

"See that girl over there sweeping the streets? That's what most untouchable children do every day – earn money so their families can survive. Without everyone working, they can't afford food. And you sit up there in your throne of gold throwing away food that is perfectly good," I say.

We continue walking, both of us in silence.

"Let's head back," I mumble.

As we walk back to the shack, Dayananda says, "I never realized how bad things are out here."

"Well you should do something about it! Help them," I say.

We finally reach the shack. We both walk in, and

Dayananda goes to rest down on the rocking chair. I go over to Ma. "Do you need me to do anything?"

"Why don't you go with Rohit to get more fruit?" She asks.

"Sure," I say, just as Rohit walks in with a pail of water. He picks up the fruit basket from the kitchen and looks at me.

"Ready?" he asks. I nod, following him out the door.

"May I join?" Dayananda asks.

"Why not?" I say, surprising myself. Rohit looks at me, puzzled.

Dayananda and I follow Rohit into the forest. We walk for a long time, over branches and dead trees. Finally, Rohit stops and puts the basket on the ground.

"Here we are!" he says. I stand by Rohit, looking up at the fruit on the trees in front of us.

"All that walking for a piece of fruit?" Dayananda pants.

"It's better than not having food at all. And it tastes

good," Rohit says as he climbs up a tree with oranges hanging from its branches.

"Right," Dayananda says, with a guilty look on his face.

I go to a different tree and start climbing. We keep picking fruit until the basket can't hold anymore.

"We should head back now," I say.

When we get back to the shack, we sit on the ground. Rohit and I eat some of our freshly picked fruit. Juice dribbles down our chins and onto to our clothes.

"Try some," I say to Dayananda. "This is all you will get for lunch."

He picks up an orange, inspects it, then peels off the skin. He looks at it again and slowly puts a piece in his mouth.

"This is so good," he says, his mouth full of orange.

Rohit and I laugh. Ma walks in with a grin on her face.

"I just heard from our neighbor that the marketplace is open again. That means the kingdom isn't under lockdown anymore. You can go home soon!" she tells Dayananda.

"This is great news! I'm very glad," he exclaims. As he stands up, he says, "I should get to the palace right away and assess the situation."

"Will you ever come by again?" Rohit asks.

"Of course I will. You have helped me so much. I don't know if I would have survived in that forest if you hadn't found me," he says.

"Oh, so you won't punish us for trying to escape?" I ask sarcastically.

"Navi. Watch your attitude," Ma warns.

"If I come back, I'll bring you guys something. Your house needs some cleaning up," Dayananda says.

"If you do, get me a nice mattress. My bed's kind of worn," I say.

"Navi!" Ma scolds.

"Sorry," I mumble.

Dayananda laughs and walks toward the door. His face falls a little bit, almost like he is sad to be leaving. Ma and Rohit walk outside with

Dayananda and I trailing behind them.

"Thank you very much for your hospitality," Dayananda says with what seems like sincere gratitude.

With that, he starts walking away, and Ma and Rohit wave. He looks back with a small smile. I head back inside with Rohit and Ma. I sit down on my bed and stare at the ground.

"Navi, can you help me clean the beds? Rohit, go to the creek and clean the dishes," Ma instructs.

And just like that, everything is back to normal, the way it used to be. But it feels wrong now. I shake out my quilt and start to lay it down on top of my bed when I see my painting, the one I gave to Dayananda. I pick it up, trying to decide what to do with it.

"Ma, I have to go. I'll be back soon," I call, running out of the shack.

"Wait! Where are you going?" she calls after me.

I run down the gravel path towards town. "Navya! Come back here!" Ma shouts.

The ground crunches beneath me, prickling my bare feet as I run. In my hurry, I forgot to put on my sandals. The sun beats down on my back, propelling me forward. At last, I reach town. Looking around wildly, I spot him walking down the path, head hung low. People whisper and point at him. Perhaps somebody recognized him. I slow down to a brisk walk and approach him, clearing my throat. He stops and turns to look at me. His face lights up when he recognizes me and he smiles.

"You forgot something," I tell him, handing him the painting.

We stay silent for a while, staring at each other as the townspeople stare at us and whisper. His eyes are on the painting, but his mind is far away.

"I'm sorry. I'll understand if you don't, but will you ever forgive me? Not just for what I did to your father, but how ignorant I've been," he asks.

"Say sorry to all the people who are suffering, not me. And fix the problem. Don't do it for me, do it because it's the right thing to do," I say.

He smiles, not paying attention to crowd gathering and whispering. "I guess I don't have any time to waste. I need to get to work."

Chapter 13

I get into a yellow kurta that Dayananda sent for me. It has tiny little mirrors shining around the neckline. It's the color of the sun and has golden borders lining the sleeves and neckline.

"Navi, hurry up! Dayananda will be expecting us." Ma yells.

I push the curtain aside that separates the washroom from the rest of our shack. Ma comes to my side, dressed in her brand new cream-colored sari. Rohit is sitting with his nose stuck in a brand-new book, dressed up in a new blue kurta. Ma smiles at me and lines my eyes with *kajal*.

"You look beautiful, Navi," she whispers.

I smooth out my dress. Today, Dayananda has called us to visit him at his palace for my birthday. The last time I saw him was when he apologized to me in town. A few days later, the messenger with the beautiful horse came by and delivered the invitation. Turns out, Ma had told Dayananda when my birthday was. I smile now, thinking about how the messenger acted when he knew we got a message from the king.

"I hate coming to this part of the kingdom," the messenger sneers in disgust, throwing a package in my direction. I catch it and turn it over. My face lights up when I see the name it.

"Do you know who this is from?" I ask.

"Of course I do. The king. I have no idea why he would want to send a letter to you, though. You live in a shack that's so small, a cricket couldn't fit in it," he says with contempt.

I open the gold package in front of him, pulling out the letter written on fancy stationary. I read what it says and laugh. My lips curl into a sly smile and I thrust it in front of the messenger's face. I let him read and it and his sneer is replaced by a look of horror.

"It looks like the king is inviting me to his palace," I say sweetly. "When I meet him, I'll be sure to tell him what a nice messenger you've been."

"I'm sorry, miss," he stammers, eyes wide, backing up to ride away in a hurry.

Ma hustles Rohit and me into the beautiful waiting carriage as I push the memory out of my mind. I play with my braid and tuck a stray piece of hair behind my ear. As the horses start towards the palace, I look around the carriage. A small picture of Dayananda decked in gold hangs behind my seat. I touch the soft seats and look out the small window, looking at my faint reflection in the glass.

"Any chance I can have one of these?" I joke.

"Really Navi?" Rohit asks, looking up from his book, a rare occurrence.

We approach the palace and Ma lets out a gasp as she stares in wonder at the outline of the majestic building. A golden flag with the kingdom's emblem waves in the wind, high in the sky, almost touching the clouds. As she gazes at the palace, I stare at the streets where untouchables beg and gawk at the carriage. Their eyes plead for food. I touch the glass of the window, wanting to help.

"Ma, can we give them the food you brought? Please?" I plead. Ma says nothing, but knocks on the inside wall of the carriage to get the charioteer's attention. She hands me the bag of food. The carriage halts. The man begins to open the door and I jump out of the carriage, running to the side of the road. Reaching into the bag, I take out some vegetables and rotis and hand a little to each of them. They gulp down the food and look up at me, grateful to have had more to eat than they may have had in days. I run back to the carriage with the empty bag and jump in. The carriage starts again.

We take a sharp turn towards the palace and stop suddenly in front of the impressive black gate. The sharp tops glint in the sunlight. I hear voices outside and then the gates open. The carriage starts moving again and stops right in front of the palace doors.

Someone opens the door of the carriage and we step out. We walk towards the doors and another guard guides us inside, through many hallways and into a large ornate room. Dayananda sits in a chair made entirely of gold and smiles when he sees us. As I look at the chair, I can't help but think of all the people who don't have food. He lifts his crown, which is embellished with rubies and emeralds, off his head and sets it down on a silver table next to his throne.

Dressed in plain clothes, he walks towards us. Instead of fabrics embroidered with gold, he wears a cotton kurta and crisp white pants with simple brown shoes.

"Happy birthday, Navya!" he wishes me. He motions for us to sit down on a bench and brings me a pile of presents. I open the first one to find new sandals made with beautiful, expensive silk.

"It looks like you've noticed how worn my sandals are," I joke.

Next, I open a package with a bunch of art supplies and a sleek new easel. I marvel at the paints and think about all the things I can create with them. "Thank you for all of this," I say.

"It's nothing," Dayananda replies. "Now, I want you to meet someone."

He introduces us to all of his family, not specifying who he wants me to meet. After we've shook hands with everyone, a new face appears at the doorway.

"There you are! You're even late to this special occasion. I shouldn't be surprised. You're late to everything," Dayananda bellows and then laughs.

A young lady races towards my family, and I realize it's Aishani, the queen's sister. She introduces herself to Ma and Rohit and then comes to me, placing her hands on my shoulders. I look up at her. She has kind green eyes.

"You must be Ram's daughter. Oh, you look so much like him. You're so pretty," Aishani says. I smile up at her.

"I was the one who wrote the letters and was trying to help you escape," she says. I take a few moments to let this new information sink in.

"But it turns out you did something way better than escape," she continues, nodding her head to Dayananda. "You changed his mind."

I frown, wondering what Aishani means, but my thoughts are interrupted. "I know you love to paint. Let me show you something," she giggles as she grabs my hand and pulls me with her.

Rohit and Ma stay behind, chatting with the other family members as Aishani guides me to the balcony. I feel a crisp breeze on my face and look down to see the whole kingdom spread out beneath me. The golden sun sets in the distance and fills the sky with magnificent bursts of pink and orange hues. The green trees are cast in a soft pinkish glow and the town beneath me is bathed in orange and gold.

Aishani leads me up more stairs, and I realize I'm standing on the very top of the palace. The winds tousle my hair around my face. I push it out of my eyes and look at the world below.

I grip the side of the wall and dare to look down at the ground. Birds soar up in the sky, gliding through the air. A boy makes his way home with a bag slung over his shoulder. A lady walks methodically, carrying a heavy pot of water on her head. As I watch, Aishani sets up an easel and art supplies.

"Care to use these?" Aishani asks with a twinkle in her eyes. I step up to the easel and do a quick sketch of the sunset and add a little color to the sky.

"You're a wonderful artist!" Aishani squeals gleefully.

"Kind of," I say.

We're quiet for a while, our thoughts lost in the beauty of the scenery. I continue sketching and use my thumb to smudge some of the sharp lines in the art.

"I feel...I feel like I should have done more, you know?" she whispers, so faintly that I wonder if I imagined it. I look up at her, and her dark, wavy hair blows in the wind. Her eyes sparkle as they fill up with tears and she purses her lips.

"Ultimately, it's my fault what happened to your father," she says, wiping a tear away with her finger. "Why am I crying? I'll never ever really understand what it's like."

I turn away from her and feel the wind against my face, blinking back my own tears.

"Look at you. I can tell how much it hurts you. I'm so, so sorry. It's easy to blame the king for this, but I'm the cause of this all. I'm sorry. I don't know how to make it right," she says.

"It's fine," I say.

"No. No, it's not. You know, at first the only reason I wanted to help you was because Ram saved my life. Now I realize how unfair the caste system is. Soon after your father was executed, I would go around untouchable neighborhoods and try to find you. That's when I saw how much they suffered. I saw how they were treated and I realized it was wrong," she says.

"Then that's all that matters," I say softly. "The fact that you realized it was wrong is what matters. Feeling pity for my family, trying to help us because Papa saved your life – those things don't matter. What matters is that you realized that the problem wasn't just our situation, it was the caste system".

We're quiet for a long time and I continue to paint. A rustle behind me makes us both turn around. Dayananda stands behind us, looking off into the distance.

"Navya," Dayananda says, turning to face me. "You have taught me many important things. You have changed me, Navya. You not only showed me what it was like living as an untouchable, you also taught me how to be kind and how to forgive. With your help, I finally realized how wrong the caste system is. You were right when you said it was unfair and limits people. Your father was right too, and I regret my decision. I've realized how horribly I have treated the people in my kingdom, and I want to change it," Dayananda says.

Dayananda holds out a golden cylinder with intricate patterns on the outside. I take it from him cautiously, feeling the weight of it in my hands. I carefully unscrew the top and a scroll slips out. I open it and read through it quickly.

"Is this real?" I ask in disbelief, my heart feeling like it might beat out of my chest.

"Yes. From this day forward, the caste system shall be banned in my kingdom. There will be no more discrimination. Untouchables can go wherever they want. They can do any job they want to do," Dayananda says with a soft smile.

I can hardly believe what I'm hearing and it takes several moments for me to process what this means. Aishani puts a hand on my arm.

"I…uh…wow. Thank you. Thank you, both of you," I stammer, tears streaming down my face.

I wrap my arms around Aishani and she hugs me back, resting her cheek on my head.

"You know, you're the one who changed him," she whispers. "I asked him if he would ban the caste system after I realized how unfair it was. He would not hear of it! After he met you, he changed."

My heart dances with joy thinking of all the people who will have a new life. I look out at the scenery and think of Papa.

Thank you, Papa. Thank you for helping me. Look at all the people you've helped me save. I couldn't have done it without you.

And I realize I am finally free. Free like a bird.

Vocabulary Words

Banyan: A tropical tree found in India that grows to be very wide and provides lots of shade.

Beta: An affectionate term used for children that means "son" or "child".

Brahmins: People of the highest and most prominent caste, Brahmins were religious leaders and teachers.

Caste system: A class structure in India that determines a person's class or status within Indian society at birth. It is made up of four different classes, ranked in order of richest to poorest. People within each class are designated to performing different jobs. The caste system has been the cause of lots of discrimination in India.

Chunni: A scarf-like garment worn around the neck.

Curry: An Indian dish that uses spices and vegetables or meat in a thick sauce and is usually served with rice or Indian bread.

Dalits (untouchables): People who are considered to be so inferior that they are not even considered to be part of the caste system. They do the most undesirable, dirty jobs in Indian society that none of the other castes want to do.

Ghagra: A floor-length skirt made of many layers of fabric. It is usually very ornate and decorated with embroidery and sometimes mirrors and bells.

Kajal: A mix of ash and oil to make eye makeup that is typically used as an eyeliner.

Kshatriyas: The caste one step below the Brahmins, Kshatriyas were warriors and people of the royal families.

Kurta: A type of knee-length shirt worn by both men and women. A kurta can be ornate or simple based on the materials and embellishments used to make it.

Langa: A floor-length skirt worn with a blouse and often decorated with embroidery.

Mango: A tropical stone fruit found in India that has a sweet and slightly tangy flavor with a smooth texture. There are many different varieties of mangoes, and not all of them have such a sweet flavor.

Roti: Tortilla like fat bread made with wheat.

Sari: A long piece of flowing fabric typically worn by adult women that is draped around the body and worn with a blouse or top.

Sudras: The caste one step below the Vaishyas, Sudras are workers and laborers.

Tamarind: A bean-like fruit found in India that has a sweet and sour taste with a sticky texture.

Teak: A tropical tree found in Asia that is often used to make furniture.

Untouchables: See Dalits.

Vaishyas: The caste one step below the Kshatriyas, Vaishyas are merchants or traders.